SOMETIMES I AM A KITE

By Kathleen A. Thompson

Illustrated by
Ilene Winn–Lederer

GREEN TIGER PRESS

Published by Simon & Schuster

NEW YORK   LONDON   TORONTO   SYDNEY   TOKYO   SINGAPORE

GREEN TIGER PRESS
Simon & Schuster Building
Rockefeller Center
1230 Avenue of the Americas
New York, New York 10020
Text copyright © 1991 by Kathleen A. Thompson
Illustrations copyright © 1991 by Ilene Winn-Lederer
All rights reserved
including the right of reproduction
in whole or in part in any form.
GREEN TIGER PRESS is an imprint of
Simon & Schuster.
Manufactured in the United States of America
10 9 8 7 6 5 4 3 2 1

Library of Congress Cataloging-in-Publication Data
Thompson, Kathleen, Sometimes I am a kite / Kathleen Thompson;
illustrated by Ilene Winn-Lederer p. cm.
Summary: As a kite is controlled by its string,
sometimes flying too high and sometimes
reeled too tight, one may draw an analogy
with human relationships as well as
the interplay of mind, body, and spirit.
I. Winn-Lederer, Ilene, ill. II. Title.
PZ7.T371597So   1991   [Fic]—dc20   90-85494   CIP
ISBN: 0-671-74789-4

To my parents, Virginia and Preston Thompson,
for their love and support,
to Karen Souders for an airborne thought,
to Richard Bach for the suggestion of a flight pattern,
and to Lawrence S. Falardeau
for helping me hold the string "just right."
—K.A.T.

For Jeff, Joshua & Ira
and the dreams we share.
—I.W.L.

Preface

If you could look down at the earth from the sky, you would see them playing. You might even faintly hear the children's voices between the sounds of surf and wind...

"May I be the kite today? Tomorrow I will hold the string for you."

"Of course. We will take turns and pass the string between us throughout our lives, and our friendship shall be our freedom and our guide."

SOMETIMES I AM A KITE . . .

. . . AND YOU HOLD THE STRING.

SOMETIMES I FLY VERY HIGH.

AND SOMETIMES YOU REEL ME IN.

WHEN YOU REEL ME IN TOO FAR,

I CANNOT SEE THE SKY OR STARS.

I HAVE NO GUIDE; I LOSE MY WAY.

BUT IF YOU GRASP THE STRING
JUST RIGHT,

WITH A LITTLE HOLD

BUT NOT TOO TIGHT . . .

... THEN I SEEM
TO KNOW MY WAY,
FREE TO FLY ABOVE
THE EARTH AND SEA,
TO SEE THE BEAUTY THAT'S
AROUND ME ...

...AND FREE TO LOVE THE ONE WHO GIVES ME THE FREEDOM TO FLY!

The text of this book is set in Goudy Bold
Display type is Minster Bold.
Designed by Judythe Sieck

ABOUT THE AUTHOR

Kathleen A. Thompson studied at Oakland Community College and Oakland University, both located in Michigan. She has worked as a writer, editor and photographer for audio-visual presentations, magazines and traveling exhibitions. *Sometimes I am a Kite* is her first children's book. Ms. Thompson lives and works in Farmington, Michigan.

ABOUT THE ILLUSTRATOR

A native of Chicago, Ilene Winn-Lederer attended the Museum School of the Art Institute of Chicago and the Chicago Academy of Fine Arts. A teacher of illustration at the Carnegie Mellon University, she is now a resident of Pittsburgh, Pennsylvania, where her work is frequently exhibited.